C700734150

D0190580

LIBRARIES NI
WITHDRAWN FROM STOCK

THE PRINCESS
AND THE
PIG

For Caroline, who knows the sort of things
that happen all the while in books - J.E.

For my friend María Oms and her love for books - P.B.

First published 2011 by Macmillan Children's Books
a division of Macmillan Publishers Limited
20 New Wharf Road, London N1 9RR
Basingstoke and Oxford
Associated companies throughout the world
www.panmacmillan.com

ISBN: 978-0-230-53141-3

Text copyright © Jonathan Emmett 2011
Illustrations copyright © Poly Bernatene 2011
Moral rights asserted.
You can find out more about Jonathan Emmett's books at
www.scribblestreet.co.uk

The inclusion of author website addresses in this book does not constitute
an endorsement by or association with Macmillan Publishers of such sites
or the content, products, advertising or other materials presented on such sites.

All rights reserved. No part of this publication may be reproduced, stored
in or introduced into a retrieval system, or transmitted, in any form, or by
any means (electronic, mechanical, photocopying, recording or otherwise)
without the prior written permission of the publisher. Any person
who does any unauthorised act in relation to this publication may be
liable to criminal prosecution and civil claims for damages.

1 3 5 7 9 8 6 4 2

A CIP catalogue record for this book is available from the British Library.

Printed in Belgium by Proost

LIBRARIES NI	
C700734150	
RONDO	26/08/2011
J	£ 10.99
COL	

THE PRINCESS
AND THE
PIG

Jonathan Emmett ★ Poly Bernatene

MACMILLAN CHILDREN'S BOOKS

N ot that long ago, in a kingdom not far
from here, a farmer was travelling home
from market with a cartload of straw.

The farmer was so poor that he didn't
have a horse and had to pull his own cart.

In the back of the cart lay
a tiny pink piglet.

Nobody wanted to buy the piglet at market,
but the farmer had taken pity on it.

"I'll call you Pigmella," he decided,
as this seemed like a good name for a pig.

It was a hot day and the farmer stopped to
rest in the shade of a great castle.
Far, far above him, on a high balcony, a queen
was inspecting her new baby daughter.

The Queen was so rich that she had **seven**
nannies and didn't have to look after her own child.

The Queen picked the baby out of her cot and held her at arm's length.

"I'll call it Priscilla," she decided, as this seemed like a good name for a princess.

A moment later, a wet squelching noise came from the baby's nappy, closely followed by an awful smell.

"Yuck!" shrieked the Queen, dropping the baby and running off to find the royal nannies.

She left so quickly that she didn't notice she had dropped the baby . . .

. . . over the **edge of the balcony!**

Down

down

down

went the baby,

into the
farmer's cart!

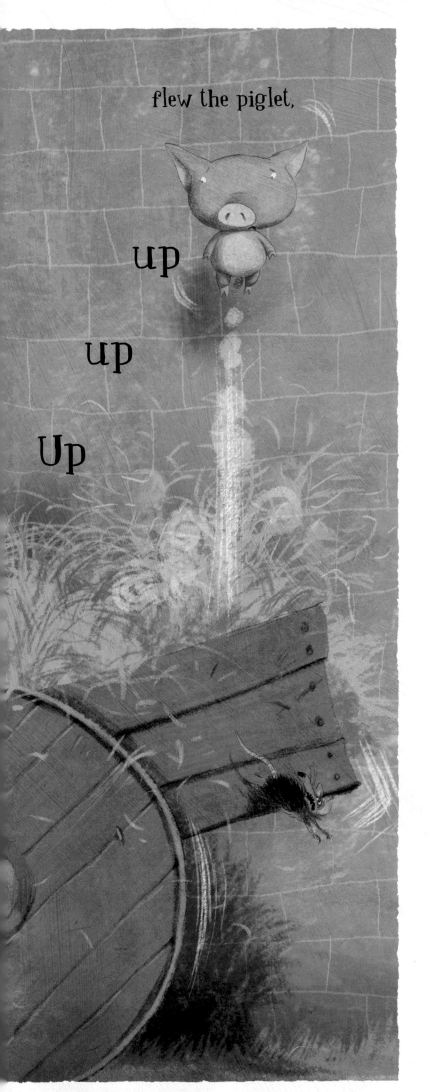

flew the piglet,

up

up

Up

into the princess's cot!

When the Queen returned and found the piglet lying where the baby should have been, she let out an even louder shriek and fainted into the nannies' arms.

The King thought he knew what had happened.

"A bad fairy has done this," he explained.
"The fairy wasn't invited to the Princess's christening,
so she's turned the baby into a piglet to get her revenge.
It's the sort of thing that happens all the while in books."

Sleeping
Beauty

Meanwhile, the farmer had
returned home and was startled
to discover a baby girl lying where
the piglet should have been.

The farmer's wife thought she knew what had happened.

"A good fairy has done this," she explained.
"The fairy knew how poor and honest we are and
how badly we want a child, so she's turned the
piglet into a baby. It's the sort of thing
that happens all the while in books."

And so, without a second thought,
the baby became Pigmella, the farmer's daughter.

And the piglet became Priscilla, the Princess.

It wasn't long before Pigmella was able to . . .

eat,

walk,

and dress, all by herself.

And the farmer and his wife soon forgot that she had ever been a pig.

Things were not so easy for Priscilla!

But the King and Queen never let anyone forget
that she was really a princess.

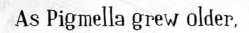

As Pigmella grew older,

she grew clever,

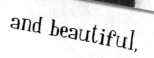

and beautiful,

and was admired
by everyone she met.

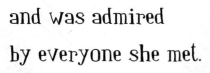

As Priscilla grew older,

she grew not so clever,

and not so beautiful,

and was avoided by **everyone** she met.

Then one day, the farmer's wife overheard some of the castle servants talking about the princess who had turned into a pig.

"It's just like what happened to Pigmella," she told her husband, "only the other way around."

THE
PRINCE
AND THE
PAUPER

The farmer soon guessed what had happened. "The Princess and the pig must have swapped places somehow," he explained. "It's the sort of thing that happens all the while in books."

The poor farmer and his wife were very unhappy. They loved Pigmella, but they knew they must return her to her rightful home.

Pigmella was also unhappy.
She loved the farmer and his wife and
did not want to live with anyone else.

But they were an honest family, so the
next day they all went to the castle to
see the King and Queen.

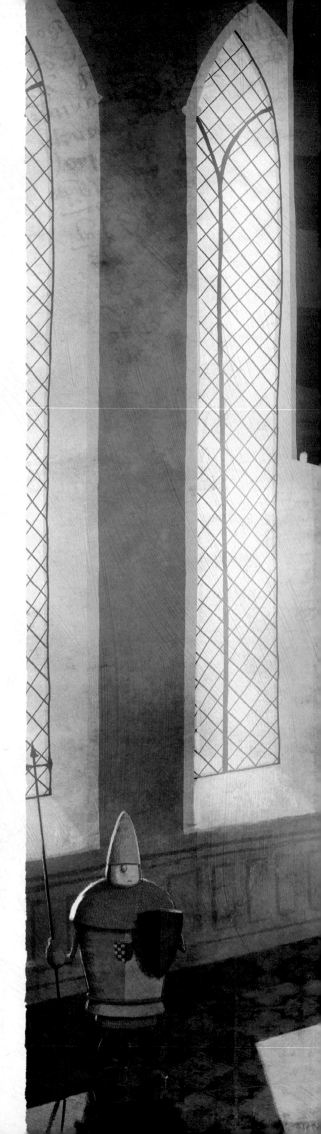

The King and Queen

listened to the farmer's story . . .

But they didn't believe it!

"What nonsense!" cried the Queen.

"Ridiculous!" laughed the King.

"This girl may be clever and beautiful,
but she does not look or speak like
a proper princess."

The Queen thought she knew what
was happening.

"It's a trick," she declared. "This girl
is just a farmer's daughter pretending
to be a princess in the hope that
she might marry a prince. It's the
sort of thing that happens all the
while in books."

Puss
in
Boots

And so Pigmella returned home with the farmer and his wife, where she married a young shepherd and lived happily ever after - and never once wished that she'd been a princess.

And Priscilla also got married – to a handsome prince!
Although he had to be talked into it.

"Priscilla was changed into a pig by a bad fairy,"
the King explained.
"But once you kiss her, the spell will be broken and she will
turn back into a beautiful princess," added the Queen.
"It's the sort of thing that happens all the while in books,"
they assured him.

But, unfortunately for the Prince . . .

. . . it's **not** the sort of thing that happens in this particular book.